To my husband, Ed—E.B.

To my mother, Marjorie Minor—W.M.

RED FOX RUNNING

by Eve Bunting

Paintings by Wendell Minor

CLARION BOOKS · NEW YORK

Red fox running,
Running through the snow,
White sky above
And white earth below.
Winter should be over,
But it didn't go away.
Hunger runs beside you
On this cold and frozen day.

Red fox stopping,

Looking up to see

A woodpecker, out of reach,

High in a tree,

Whooper swans huddled

Where the lake shines through,

An eagle, silent in the air,

His shadow silent too.

Red fox, hungry fox,

Listening to hear

The scrabble scrabble scrabble

Of a white-tailed deer,

The rustle of the cranes

As they lift into the sky,

The sad, lonely echo

Of a last loon's cry.

Red fox, starving fox,

Desperate to find

A rabbit or a rodent,

Food of any kind.

Night is coming faster now,

The world is turning gray,

Edges blur and darkness crawls

Along the end of day.

Red fox, weary fox,

Slinking down to creep

Low in the hollow

Where the snow lies deep,

Wary of a wildcat

That's belly-creeping, too —

A fast and famished wildcat

That may be watching you!

Red fox, joyous fox,

Sniffing what you've found,

Dragging it behind you

Along the frosty ground.

Your paws are raw and bleeding,

Your body's sore and spent.

You stumble round in circles,

At last you find your scent.

The lake of ice is shining,

The moon's an orange glow,

The falling stars are streaks of flame,

So far, so far to go.

But here's a rock,

A stump of tree,

A smell you recognize.

You find new strength to stagger on,

To hurry with your prize.

Red fox, red fox,

Crawl into your den.

Food for you,

Your mate and cubs,

Eat your fill and then

All curled together

In a warm, furry heap,

Sleep safely, red fox,

Sleep, sleep, sleep.

EVE BUNTING, one of Clarion's most acclaimed and versatile authors, was born and educated in Ireland. She has written a wide variety of books for Clarion, ranging from holiday stories such as *The Mother's Day Mice* and *The Day Before Christmas* to the sensitive and moving story of a homeless boy in *Fly Away Home*. The concern for nature Ms. Bunting expresses in *Red Fox Running* is also evident in her most recent Clarion picture book, *Someday a Tree*, about the fate of a beloved oak. Eve Bunting lives in Pasadena, California.

WENDELL MINOR was born in Aurora, Illinois, and was educated at the Ringling School of Art and Design in Florida. He is well known for his paintings featured on book jackets and in picture books. His work includes *Sierra, Heartland,* and *Mojave*, all by Diane Siebert, *The Seashore Book* by Charlotte Zolotow, and *The Moon of the Owls* by Jean Craighead George. He is the recipient of over two hundred professional awards. Mr. Minor lives in Washington, Connecticut, with his wife, Florence, and their two cats, Willie and Mouse.

Clarion Books   a Houghton Mifflin Company imprint   215 Park Avenue South, New York, NY 10003   Text copyright © 1993 by Eve Bunting   Illustrations copyright © 1993 by Wendell Minor   The illustrations in this book were painted with gouache and watercolor on cold-press watercolor board.   All rights reserved.   For information about permission to reproduce selections from this book, write to Permissions, Houghton Mifflin Company, 215 Park Avenue South, New York, NY 10003.   www.houghtonmifflinbooks.com   Printed in China.   Library of Congress Cataloging-in-Publication Data   Bunting, Eve, 1928– Red Fox running / Eve Bunting ; illustrated by Wendell Minor   p. cm.   Summary: Rhyming text follows the experiences of a red fox as it searches across a wintry landscape for food.   ISBN: 0-395-58919-3   [1. Red fox—Fiction. 2. Foxes—Fiction. 3. Stories in rhyme.]   I. Minor, Wendell, ill. II. Title. PZ8.3.B92Re   1993   [E]—dc20   92-27   CIP AC

CL ISBN-13: 978-0-395-58919-9   CL ISBN-10: 0-395-58919-3   PA ISBN-13: 978-0-395-79723-5   PA ISBN-10: 0-395-79723-3

SCP 10 9 8 7 6 5 4